Sunrise, Sunset

LYRICS BY **Sheldon Harnick** ~ MUSIC BY **Jerry Bock**

ILLUSTRATED BY **Ian Schoenherr**

HarperCollinsPublishers

For Charlotte and Sam

Is this the little girl I carried?
Is this the little boy at play?

I don't remember growing older.
When did they?

When did she get to be a beauty?
When did he grow to be so tall?

Wasn't it yesterday

when they were small?

Sunrise, sunset,
Sunrise, sunset,
Swiftly flow the days;

Seedlings turn overnight to sunflow'rs,

Blossoming even as we gaze.

Sunrise, sunset,
Sunrise, sunset,
Swiftly fly the years;

One season following another,

Laden with happiness and tears.

Now is the little boy a bridegroom,
Now is the little girl a bride.

Under the canopy I see them,
Side by side.

Place the gold ring around her finger,
Share the sweet wine and break the glass;
Soon the full circle will have come to pass.

Sunrise, sunset,
Sunrise, sunset,
Swiftly flow the days;

Seedlings turn overnight to sunflow'rs,
Blossoming even as we gaze.

Sunrise, sunset,
Sunrise, sunset,
Swiftly fly the years;

One season following another,
Laden with happiness and tears.

Sunrise, Sunset

LYRICS BY **Sheldon Harnick** ~ MUSIC BY **Jerry Bock**

Moderately Slow Waltz tempo (soulful and wistful)

Is this the lit‑tle girl I car — ried? Is this the lit‑tle boy at
Now is the lit‑tle boy a bride — groom, Now is the lit‑tle girl a

play? I don't re — mem‑ber grow — ing old — er. When
bride. Un — der the can — o — py I see them, Side

did they?_____ When did she get to be a beau — ty?
by side._____ Place the gold ring a — round her fin — ger,

When did he grow to be so tall? Was‑n't it
Share the sweet wine and break the glass; Soon the full

yes‑ter‑day when they were small?_____
cir‑cle will have come to pass._____

Sunrise, Sunset • Text and music © 1964, renewed 1992, by Mayerling Productions Ltd. and Jerry Bock
Enterprises • Text and music © renewed and assigned to R & H Music c/o Mayerling Productions Ltd. and
to Robinson, Brog, Leinwand, Greene, Genovese & Gluck P.C. • Illustrations copyright © 2005 by Ian
Schoenherr • Manufactured in China. • All rights reserved. • www.harperchildrens.com

Library of Congress Cataloging-in-Publication Data Harnick, Sheldon. Sunrise, sunset / lyrics by Sheldon
Harnick; music by Jerry Bock; illustrated by Ian Schoenherr. — 1st ed p. cm. Summary: An illustrated
version of the well-known song about the passage of time, from the musical "Fiddler on the Roof."
ISBN 0-06-051525-2 — ISBN 0-06-051527-9 (lib. bdg.) 1. Children's songs, English—United States—Texts.
[1. Songs.] I. Bock, Jerry. II. Schoenherr.
Ian, ill. III. Title. PZ8.3.H2183Su 2005   2004019104   782.42—dc22   CIP   [E] AC
Typography by Martha Rago 1 2 3 4 5 6 7 8 9 10 • First Edition
Printed in China
0422/ B1083/A1